W9-CFB-595

Lisa ran around her backyard. She was busy looking at the flowers, sky, and plants. It felt good to be outside on days when she felt strong. So many days she felt sick.

Lisa noticed a milkweed plant with a small creature on one of its big leaves. Curious, she crept closer.

"It's a caterpillar!" Lisa exclaimed. She loved caterpillars and butterflies.

"Hello," the creature answered, "who are you?"

"Hey, you can talk!" Lisa laughed delightedly. "I'm Lisa. Do you have a name?"

"No, but I'd like to," the caterpillar answered hopefully.

"Good! I'll name you 'Sonya,'" said Lisa.

"Why Sonya?" the caterpillar sounded puzzled.

"Because I once had a good friend named Sonya," Lisa explained.

"What happened to her?" Sonya asked. "Did you love her?"

"Oh yes," said Lisa, "but she had cancer and died."

"What's died?" Sonya asked.

"Well, I asked my mom," said Lisa. "She said when you die your body stops working. It doesn't breathe, hear, see, or feel anything."

"Then what happens?" asked Sonya curiously.

"Mom says your spirit leaves your body and you change," Lisa explained. "Dying happens to all living things. It just happens to some a little sooner—like it did to my friend."

"Does it hurt?" asked Sonya.

"I don't think so. I just know that you change," Lisa said matter-of-factly.

"That's funny," said Sonya. "I have strange feelings inside me. Am I going to change? Does that mean I'm going to die?"

"Oh no, I don't think so," Lisa assured her. "You're a caterpillar and caterpillars change into something else—butterflies!"

"What are butterflies?" asked Sonya.

Lisa smiled. "Oh, they're beautiful! They have lovely wings and they fly up against the blue sky, and when they get thirsty, they go to the flowers and drink their juice."

Sonya shook her head. "That sounds nice, but do you really think I will change into a butterfly?"

"Oh, I'm sure," said Lisa, "I wish I could be one."

"Why?"

"Because, I have cancer, like my friend Sonya did, and if I were a butterfly, maybe I could fly away from my sickness and then I wouldn't feel so bad."

Sonya looked puzzled. "What is it like to be sick?" she asked.

"Oh, after I get my medicine, I feel sick to my stomach for a while," Lisa answered. "But it goes away. Sometimes I get tired too."

"Well, if being sick is anything like I feel inside me, maybe you're going to be a butterfly too," said Sonya.

Lisa giggled. "People don't change into butterflies. At least, I don't think they do."

Then they heard a voice call, "Lisa! Lisa!"

"Oh, that's my mom. I've got to go in, take my medicine, and have some lunch," explained Lisa.

"What do you eat for lunch?" Sonya asked.

"Usually a sandwich with cookies and milk. I have to keep up my strength. Do you want some?" Lisa offered.

"No, I'll just stay here and stuff myself with this leaf," said Sonya. "See, I eat and get fat, then I get a new skin."

Lisa looked doubtful. "Sometimes I get puffy, but I never get a new skin. I'll see you after lunch." She ran into the house.

After lunch Lisa brought her mom out to meet Sonya.

"See, Mom, this is Sonya, my new friend," she announced.

Lisa's mom looked at Sonya. "Lisa, she will turn into a butterfly," she said, "but not just any kind of butterfly."

"Hear that, Sonya? What kind will she turn into?" Lisa asked.

Mom smiled as she looked at Sonya. "Well, she's going to be a Monarch butterfly. They migrate here from Mexico and they are big, beautiful, orange and black butterflies. They live on milkweed plants like the one Sonya is eating."

"Hey, Sonya, you had your milk for lunch too!" Lisa laughed.

As Lisa's mother turned to go back in the house, she said, "Take a close look at Sonya. She's really a pretty caterpillar!"

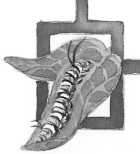

"Pretty? I don't feel pretty, I feel ugly!" Sonya humphed.

"Me too. Look." Lisa took off her cap. "I don't have any hair."

"Why not?" Sonya asked.

"Cause the medicine I take makes me lose my hair," Lisa explained.

"Well, I don't have any hair and you think I'm pretty. Do you think if you ate milkweed you would look like me?" Sonya asked.

Lisa giggled. "That's a funny idea."

Sonya sat and chomped on her leaf for awhile. Lisa stared at the sky and then at Sonya.

"Lisa, you're so quiet," Sonya remarked.

"I know, I need quiet times to think," Lisa said.

"What are you thinking about?" Sonya asked.

"Well, I was watching you and hoping you wouldn't go away and that I could see you turn into a butterfly," she explained.

"Oh, I won't leave," said Sonya. "Unless some other caterpillar comes along to eat on this plant. There isn't enough food for two caterpillars. What else are you thinking?"

"I was just hoping that they would find a cure for my sickness. I'm . . . afraid," Lisa said quietly.

"Me too," said Sonya. "I like you."

"Would you tell me how you feel as you are changing?" Lisa asked.

"Sure," said Sonya. "Will you stay with me to cheer me up?"

"Oh, yes. But I have to go to the hospital tomorrow for a check-up. Will you be here when I get back?" Lisa asked.

"Of course I will," said Sonya. "You're my friend!"

Two days later when Lisa returned from the hospital, she went immediately out into the yard to look for Sonya. "Sonya!" she called. "Sonya! Sonya!"

"Here I am," said Sonya. "But I feel terrible."

"What's the matter?" Lisa looked at her carefully to see if she was sick too.

"I feel like my skin is getting thin, and I'm going to lose it again," said Sonya.

"Oh. That must be like me losing my hair all the time," said Lisa. "But something else is wrong, isn't it?"

"Yes," said Sonya. "There's another caterpillar on my plant. I'm too weak to fight for the food."

"I see it! Oh, that's terrible. But it needs to live too," said Lisa. She paused. "I've got problems too," she said sadly. "I've got to go back into the hospital. Maybe for a long time. My cancer isn't getting better."

Sonya started to cry. "So...so I won't be seeing you anymore?" she asked.

Lisa started to cry too.

"I guess not...I guess I'm going to...lose another friend!" Lisa ran back into the house, sobbing as she went.

Later that evening Lisa brought her dad out into the yard to see Sonya. "See, Daddy! There she is and over there is the other caterpillar. There's not enough food for both of them," she pointed out.

"Maybe we can do something to help Sonya. Let's look for another milkweed plant for the other caterpillar to eat," her dad said.

Bright and early the next morning, Lisa and her mom and dad went out into the field behind their house and found another milkweed plant. Carefully they picked up the other caterpillar and its leaf from Sonya's plant and put it on the new milkweed plant.

As they went back into the house, Dad said, "Sonya should be all right now."

The day Lisa left for the hospital was bright and beautiful, but Lisa didn't feel bright and beautiful. She had said goodbye to her friend Sonya the night before, but she was afraid she would never see her again.

"Dad, could I please say goodbye to Sonya, one more time?" she asked.

"No, Lisa. We have to leave," he answered.

"But Daddy—"

"Everything is loaded in the car. We have to go," said Dad. They piled into the car and left for the hospital.

The hospital was big, but friendly. Lisa liked her doctor, John, and her nurse, Jan. She especially liked the physician's assistant Jerry—he didn't have any hair, just like her.

When she got to her room, her mother arranged her clothes and all her games. But Lisa still looked sad and scared.

Her mom noticed. "You look sad, honey."

"I am," said Lisa, "I miss Sonya."

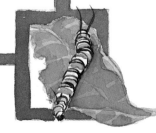

"Hi, Lisa, look what I have!" Dad called, standing in the doorway.

He was holding a big pot, and guess what was in it? That's right—a milkweed plant! And guess who was on one of the leaves? Sonya!

"I want you to know your doctor and I picked out just the right room so the plant would have enough light to keep growing for your hungry friend here," said Dad.

"Oh, thank you, Dad." Lisa smiled happily. She hugged her mother. "I'll be all right now," she said.

The next morning when Lisa woke up, Sonya was waiting for her.

"Lisa, I'm so glad to be here, but..." Sonya hesitated.

"But what?" Lisa prodded.

"But something is happening to me," Sonya said slowly. "I don't feel like I'm going to be here very long."

Lisa watched as silky white fluid began to come out of Sonya's mouth. And in the manner that has happened for thousands of years, Sonya began to make a small pad of the white fluid. She placed it underneath the leaf she was sitting on. Then she put her back feet on the pad of silk.

Lisa asked, "Sonya, what are you doing? How do you know to do that?"

"I don't know, it's like I've always known what I was supposed to do," said Sonya.

"What are you doing now?" Lisa asked. "You're upside down."

"I feel better this way. Somehow, I just know this is how it's supposed to be," she answered.

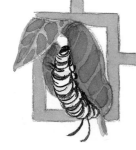

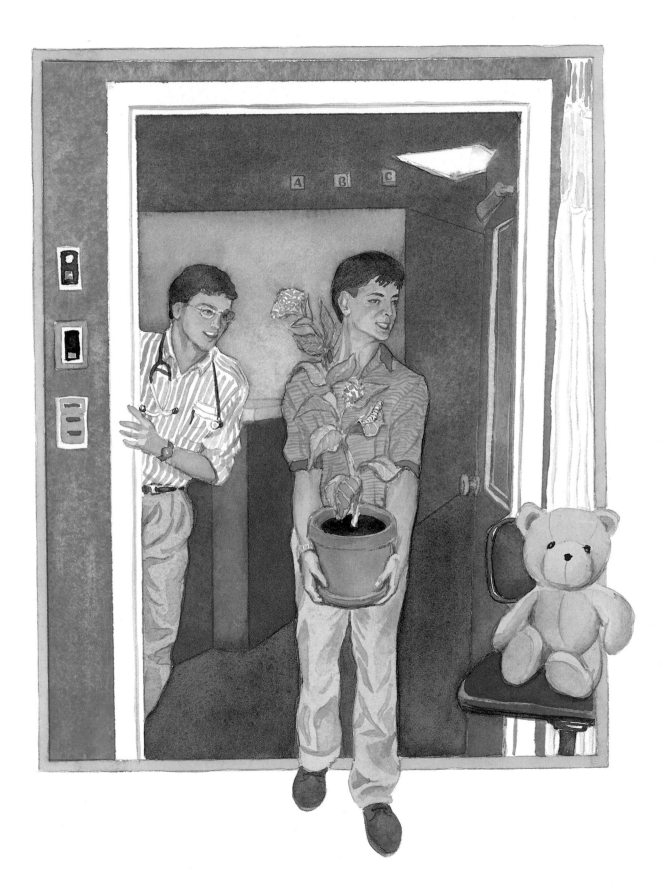

Then Sonya, with her back feet held securely by the pad of silk, started to curl her long body up to meet her feet. She looked like a letter "J" as she struggled to make her ends meet. Her old skin, so very thin, began to sluff off and underneath Lisa could see her new skin—it was a beautiful turquoise color with silver designs.

"Oh, Sonya," Lisa exclaimed. "You're becoming a chrysalis!"

"A what?" Sonya asked, puzzled.

"A chrysalis," Lisa repeated, excitedly. "It's how you'll change into a butterfly."

"I'm scared," Sonya said, "I don't seem to have any control over what's happening."

"Tell me what it feels like," Lisa urged.

"It feels...strange. I can't move too well, and I feel weak, but I want to be strong. And I'm sleepy, but I'm afraid to sleep. My eyes want to close, but I want to see you...." Sonya's voice faded.

"You'll be all right," said Lisa. "You'll go to sleep for a while, and when you wake up you'll be a butterfly—not just an ordinary butterfly, but a beautiful Monarch butterfly!"

"Are you sure?" Sonya asked, her voice distant and weak.

"Yes, I'm positive. And do you know what? Dr. John says that all along you've been taking your medicine too, just like me, because milkweed has medicine in it. So you see, you took your medicine to help you live to become a chrysalis. Oh, you're so beautiful," Lisa said happily. She called one last time, "Sonya!"

But Sonya didn't hear Lisa. She was all wrapped up in her turquoise and silver world of would-be dreams.

The days seemed long to Lisa without Sonya. She counted the days until Sonya would reappear as a butterfly.

First day...second day....

Lisa began to feel worse and worse. She felt weak. It was hard to smile.

Dr. John came in her room. "Look, Lisa, you have to think positively. We need you to help us if you're going to get well."

"I know, Dr. John, I try," she said.

Then Jerry, the physician's assistant, came in. "Hey, I tell you jokes and you don't laugh? You've got to shape up. Feel good. Get back on top of the world!" He smiled encouragingly.

"I'm trying, Jerry, really I am," Lisa said.

Lisa's nurse, Jan, visited too. She hugged Lisa, gave her medicine and held her hand.

Finally the day came when Lisa's mom and dad packed all her things in the car, including Sonya, and took Lisa home. She was still sick, but she was going home.

Lisa sat in between her parents in the car. She felt sleepy, but she'd been wondering about something.

"Mom, Dad," she said, "what happens after you die?" There was a short silence. Lisa's dad reached for her hand. Her mom put an arm around her shoulders.

"Well, honey," said her dad, "different people believe different things. Grandpa always said that when he died, he was going to be with God in a beautiful place called heaven."

"I think that when we die, we change," said Mom. "We won't feel pain anymore and we'll be beautiful and peaceful. What is for sure though, Lisa, is that we will always love you—and when someone loves you, you are never alone."

"That's good," said Lisa. "I'll always love you too."

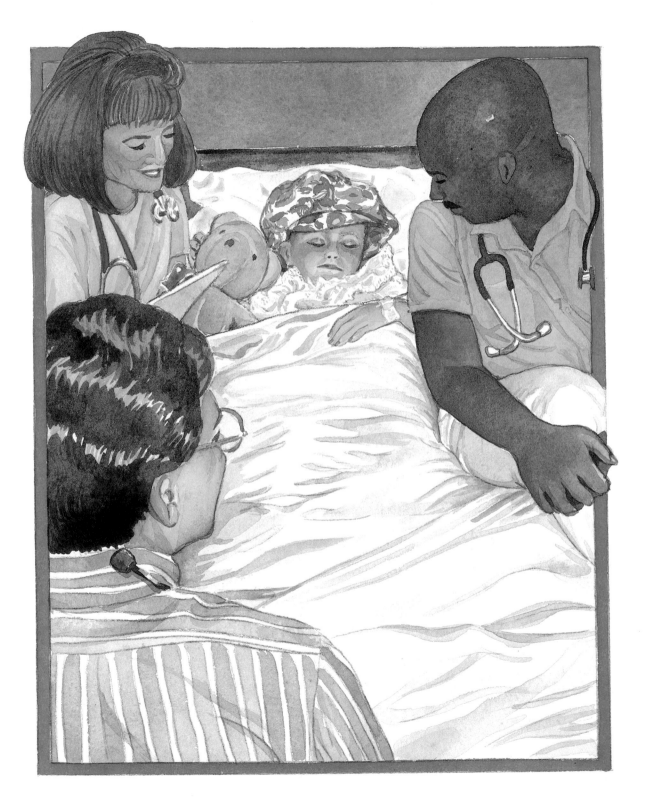

The days passed...six, seven, eight....

Then one morning, Lisa said, "Mom, you know, I think I feel just like Sonya did when she went into her chrysalis. It's hard for me to move. I feel so weak, and I'm sleepy, but I'm afraid to sleep. I can't help...feeling...that... something...big is happening."

"Lisa, maybe today will be the day that Sonya comes out," said Mom. "Look, see how the chrysalis has become transparent. You can see the darkness of the butterfly inside."

"Yes, and I just can't wait. I'm so afraid I won't see her." Lisa felt very tired.

Dad came in the room and sat down on the bed. "We all want to see Sonya," he said.

They waited and watched.

Pretty soon there was a stirring, and more stirring, and twisting, and suddenly Dad said, "Look, Lisa!" Lisa turned her head slowly and looked.

Out of the chrysalis emerged a strange creature. It looked long and black and wet. It didn't look like a butterfly at all.

"Oh, Sonya. I'm so glad you made it, even though you don't exactly look like a butterfly," Lisa said, smiling weakly.

It wasn't too long before the creature moved and began to unfold the wings that had been hidden in its darkness. It couldn't fly yet. Its wings were too wet, but the butterfly looked at Lisa.

"She knows me. I told her she'd make it," Lisa sighed. "Now, I can go to sleep too."

Lisa closed her eyes. They were very heavy and it felt sooooo good to rest them. Then the heaviness in her eyes and her body slowly slipped away, and a wonderful lightness, like air on a spring day, replaced it. She felt like sunshine. Then the strangest thing happened. Lisa felt as if she was floating. She felt high in the air. She looked down to see if she really was. And sure enough, she could see her body lying in her bed. And she could see her mom and dad sitting on the side of the bed. She called out to them, but they didn't seem to hear. Instead, her mom bent over the bed and began to cry.

"Mom! Mom! Don't cry. Look at me! I'm floating! Up here! I feel wonderful, Mom!" she called.

They couldn't hear her but she somehow knew, just like Sonya, that all of this was supposed to happen.

Lisa's mom, still crying, left the room. Her dad stayed. He bent over Lisa, covered her with the blanket and kissed her. Then he went over and picked up Sonya whose wings were still wet, and put her on the sill by the open window. He thought he was the only one to see Sonya stretch her wings for the first time.

But Lisa saw. And from her high perch, she lightly called, "Sonya, Sonya!"

Her father turned and left. But Sonya turned around and looked inquiringly back into the room. "Where are you?" she asked.

"I'm here, up here. And I feel wonderful!" Lisa laughed. "How do you feel? You look beautiful."

"I feel light. I feel like I could fly, and I will." Sonya stretched her regal orange and black wings.

"May I fly with you?" Lisa asked.

"Of course, you may," said Sonya. "Come ride on my wings and we'll climb up into the sky together."

Lisa had only to think about it, and she felt herself move through space toward Sonya. She felt the softness of butterfly wings beneath her and then, a rush of air, and blueness...blueness...blueness....

Lisa's mom cried when she called the doctor to tell him that Lisa died. He cried, too, when he told Jan and Jerry.

Later that day Jan went home. She felt very sad. She wanted time alone to think about Lisa, so she decided to do some weeding in her garden.

A Monarch butterfly landed on the stone step next to her. Jan smiled sadly, remembering Lisa. When she went to the other side of the house, the butterfly followed her. Then, when she returned to the garden, the butterfly followed her again, this time landing on her finger. Gently, Jan took the butterfly over to the birdbath and gave it a drink. The butterfly paused for a moment, spread its beautiful wings, and fluttered around her head. Then like a feather on the wind, it rose, parting the blue sky with its golden wings, and was gone.

Jerry, too, was sad. He had wanted to say good-bye to Lisa. He went home and looked out his kitchen window into the backyard. It was fresh and green, alive with plants and flowers—"just like I remember Lisa," he thought, "alive, bright, and beautiful. But wait!" He thought, "What is that?"

Jerry ran out of the house. He couldn't believe his eyes. Hundreds of Monarch butterflies swarmed around him! They lingered in the yard as he watched them. Just as they were about to leave, one beautiful Monarch flew over and fluttered around his head. It kissed his cheek with its wing and flew away.

Two days later, Lisa's mom called Jan to thank her and the rest of the staff for all their kindness to Lisa. She added, "It was so strange. After we said good-bye to Lisa at the funeral, we came home to find our whole backyard flooded with sunshine and filled with glorious orange, black and yellow Monarch butterflies.

"And down where the milkweed plant used to grow, one lone butterfly was gliding on a little breeze. We walked toward it and it fluttered up to meet us. It danced on light-filled wings in front of our faces. It touched us and then, as if it had heard some far-off call, it turned and soared up and up into the blue sky.

"And we waved to it...Good-bye."

ILLUSTRATOR'S DEDICATION

To Shayla

AUTHOR'S DEDICATION

This story is fiction based on
the actual experience of
Jan Luzins and Jerry Janiec.

It is dedicated with love to:

Jeff Block

Bonnie Freeman

Rachael Green

Tracy Henshaw

Sean Hollis

Lisa Perras

Sonya Gradsky,

with a special tribute to
Dr. John Graham-Pole whose
love and dedication to children
has brought butterflies into the
lives of many. I also wish to
thank Patricia Lehnen for her
efforts and undying belief
in the story.

AFTERWORD

Was it just a coincidence? The very day that Marilyn Maple's poignant story arrived for me to read, I also received a magnificent painting of a young child gazing reflectively upon a butterfly! The painting, by Marilyn Sunderman, was a gift and Appreciation Award from The Compassionate Friends, an international organization of bereaved parents.

For children of all ages, the butterfly symbolizes hope, faith, and reassurance. It is no coincidence that in Holocaust literature, discovered after the liberation of the concentration camps, were youngsters' immortal poems now inscribed forever in our own literature: *Butterflies Are Free* and *I Never Saw Another Butterfly*.

Children are more aware of dying and death than most adults realize. Of course, the ability to understand this reality depends not only upon age, but upon the social and environmental support of the family. We cannot, and should not, shield children from its reality. Understanding death is a life-long process that stretches from childhood to old age. Death education begins when life begins. *On the Wings of a Butterfly* will become an indispensable tool for coping in the face of on-coming loss.

As we read this compelling and insightful book, let us stay close to our youngsters. Hug them so they feel our warmth and love. What is said is significant, but *how* it is said will communicate more eloquently than specific words.

Let us remember that theology cannot merely be taught, but must be caught. Keep the door ajar to their doubts, questions, and differences of opinion. Respect their individuality, for in the long run, they must find their own answers to the questions of life and death.

The greatest challenge will not be explaining dying and death to children, but how to make peace with it ourselves.

Rabbi Earl A. Grollman, D.D.
Author of *Talking About Death: A Dialogue Between Parent and Child*

NOTE FROM THE AUTHOR

This is a story about Lisa, a real little girl whose love of and belief in butterflies as a beautiful symbol of on-going life touched the lives of all those who knew her.

This book is the result of a promise I made to the many children who asked me to write a book about death. Children who must confront a terminal illness are very brave. Most of them, in trying to ease the burden for their parents, deny their own fears of death. However, they will often discuss their needs with someone outside the family. This can help them to obtain a visual image, a belief, or a hope, to bridge the confining cocoon of illness to a rebirth into a new form of life. Health professionals confirm that children suffering serious illness cling to one or two symbols of eternity—such as rainbows and butterflies.

Healthy children today are often confronted by death very early in life. Children are dying of AIDS, of prenatal and personal drug abuse, and many other diseases for which we have names but no cures.

Because of the increasing numbers of youthful deaths, and because we are becoming more open about discussing death and grief, teachers are finding they need to integrate the concept of death as a part of the life cycle into the classroom.

Lisa's story is meant to encourage discussion about the normal process of dying as it relates to the continuation of life. This story attempts to open the doors of communication with children about their own religious perceptions and their family's religious persuasion or tradition—especially about such topics as life after death. All major religions in the world believe in some form of life after death. For those who have no such religious belief, a knowledge of science points to life as an on-going process.

I hope the story of Lisa and the butterflies will provide comfort for children who are ill. It can provide enlightenment for children who are learning about life's cycles. Parents can find here an impetus for communicating their beliefs and values. I hope it will provide an opportunity for religious teachers to interpret concepts and discuss death with children. And I hope teachers will use the story to help children who have to confront the death of a classmate.

In support of all of you, may Lisa, Sonya, and all those who have died live on through you and the butterflies.

Marilyn Maple, Ph.D.
Gainesville, Florida

Talking with children about sensitive topics...

isn't always easy. With books from Parenting Press, you can address issues like death, feelings, and other difficult subjects with grace and sensitivity.

On the Wings of a Butterfly: A Story about Life and Death

Written by Marilyn Maple, Ph.D.

This is a gentle, affirming story about Lisa, a young child with cancer. Seeking to make sense of her own mortality, Lisa befriends Sonya, a caterpillar preparing for transformation into a monarch butterfly, and the two support each other through their journeys of changes. The story provides a generous, uplifting start for talking with children—and listening to them talk—about the cycles of life and death.

$9.95 paper. $18.95 hardcover, illustrated

Dealing with Feelings

Written by Elizabeth Crary

Especially in times of crisis or conflict, children need help with identifying and expressing their feelings.   At the best of times, feelings are hard to understand. Sensing tension or sadness about events in their world can multiply this confusion. This series for children ages 3-9 models creative, non-destructive ways children can express specific emotions.

Each: $5.95 paper. $16.95 library binding, illustrated

I'm Mad

When rain cancels a long-awaited picnic, Katie announces, "I'll be mad and mean all day!" Katie's dad encourages her to think of creative, non-destructive ways to express herself.

I'm Frustrated

Alex's older brother and sister can skate effortlessly. It looks so easy, but he can't do it! How can he cope with his frustration? Your child decides in a no-risk setting.

I'm Proud

Bursting with pride, Mandy runs to tell her family she can tie her shoes...only to find that no one is very impressed. Your child will help Mandy find ways to value herself and her achievement.

See your bookseller, or contact
Parenting Press,
P.O. Box 75267, Seattle, WA 98125,
or call 800-992-6657